Ivy

by Anthony Masters

Illustrated by Ian Miller

Introduction

When Barry follows his dog into the ivy-covered cottage, he is very scared.

"Spot!"
The little dog was whimpering now.
"Spot!"
Then Barry saw him crouching before a half-open door. There was something in there that was making poor Spot terrified. What could it be?

Now read on to find out the secret of the cottage.

CHAPTER 1

The Ivy-covered Cottage

The ivy rustled and tapped at the windows in a horrible way.

Barry had never seen anything like it. Old Mrs Hudson's cottage was being strangled by the stuff. All the walls and windows as well as the front door were covered. It was even starting to spread over the roof.

He stood in the lane and stared, feeling scared. A little wind was making the ivy move to and fro like hundreds of snakes. Then Barry realized there wasn't any wind. The afternoon was completely still, so what was making the ivy rattle?

Barry shuddered and ran back to his gran's house as fast as he could.

He didn't like the country. It was boring, and when it wasn't boring it was scary. The owls seemed to hoot all night.

He missed his mates and the town, with its ice-rink and skateboarding. There was nothing to do in the country. Even his roller boots wouldn't work on the cracked surface of the narrow lanes. But Barry knew he had to make the best of it. His mum was ill so he had to stay with Gran.

While he was eating his tea, Barry
asked his gran about the ivy-covered
cottage. Although he didn't say he'd been
scared, she guessed it. She looked worried.

"You should keep away from there,"
said Gran uneasily.

"Why?" He almost sounded rude, but he wanted to know more about the creepy place. Barry grinned inside. Creepy? That described the ivy really well.

"It's lonely down there."

"Just lonely?"

"Yes." Gran's eyes didn't quite meet his.

"I've never seen so much ivy." Barry was trying to prod her into telling him all she knew.

"Mrs Hudson had one of the best gardens in the district," said Gran.

"She fought the ivy all her life. She tried to cut it down, but it always grew back."

"Is she dead?" asked Barry.

"No. She got too old to cope. At least, that's what they say in the village. She went to Canada to live with an old friend. She didn't have any children."

"What else did she do to the ivy?"

Barry was trying to imagine the old lady's battle against the creeping plant. He was beginning to feel sorry for her.

"They say she used every kind of spray – and she even tried to burn some of it. But the ivy wouldn't go away."

Gran got up and began to stack the plates. "It's not a nice place, that cottage," she said. "And I don't want you going back there."

That was enough for Barry. Once anyone warned him off like that they gave him an urge to go ahead.

Barry was always daring himself to do things he didn't want to do – and each time he did them he got into trouble.

That night, as he tried to sleep, he remembered how he had gone into a spooky old warehouse and been caught by a security guard. Another time he had climbed on to the roof of the school and been in big trouble with the head teacher. He was small for his age, but he wanted to be tough.

Now he would have to go back to Mrs Hudson's cottage. He shivered. He didn't want to go there. But he knew he would have to.

CHAPTER 2

Nightmare

That night Barry dreamt of running away
from Mrs Hudson's cottage with the ivy
rustling after him. It was shooting out
stems along the lane, trying to trap his feet
and to wind itself round his legs.

Barry kept running. The ivy was centimetres away from him when he got back to Gran's house. He tore up to his room, slammed the door and pulled a

chest of drawers against it, but the ivy was
climbing up the sides of the house. He
could hear it rattling and tapping at the
windows.

Barry woke suddenly. He was trembling. Then he heard the scratching sound at the door.

He lay there, too terrified to move. The ivy was coming to get him. Then he heard a gentle whine and realized it was only Spot, Gran's little black-and-white terrier.

Barry opened the door and let him in. Then he went back to bed; Spot jumped up on the blankets, licking his face. As he stroked the dog, he made up his mind. He wasn't going to let a load of old ivy give him nightmares. He'd go down and face it out this morning. If he took Spot with him for company, Barry was sure he wouldn't be so scared.

CHAPTER 3

Into the Cottage

But Barry *was* scared. When he got to the cottage the ivy looked even more snake-like than before. Spot began to bark.

"Wait!" Barry yelled.

But Spot had dived through the only space the ivy hadn't covered – an open trapdoor that must lead down to the cellar.

"Spot," he yelled. "Spot, come back at once."

But the dog didn't.

"Spot!"

Then he heard the barking from somewhere inside the cottage.

"Spot!"

The ivy began to rustle in a horrible way, but, once again, there wasn't the slightest breath of wind. Spot's barking turned into an awful howl, and then a frightened yelping.

The hairs on Barry's neck began to stiffen. He knew what he had to do. He had to go inside.

Barry only just fitted through the trapdoor. He had to wriggle and push and shove.

A strand of ivy got caught around his ankle at the last moment and he panicked. The more he struggled, the tighter its grip seemed to grow until it was really hurting.

He kicked hard. The ivy snapped and he fell on to the cellar floor. Choking and gasping he sat up.

The rustling was all round him as if he was in a tree rather than the pitch black cellar of a cottage. He could still hear Spot howling. Barry got up and began to feel his way round the walls. They were covered in spiders' webs and their sticky threads clung to his fingers. Something

soft and leggy ran under his arm and he
screamed. Barry couldn't bear spiders.

At last he found the door, but at first
he couldn't lift the latch. Then he grabbed
it in both hands, pushing it up with a loud
click. Barking fiercely, Spot rushed past
him.

Barry slowly climbed a flight of stone steps and found himself in the kitchen. It was bathed in a dim, green light and felt a bit like being underwater. The ivy had broken through the glass in the windows. It lay across the floor in long strands

which seemed to move slightly as Barry stepped over them.

Then one tendril caught his ankle again. This time he fell over on the dusty cracked lino where another tendril caught round his wrist. Both began to squeeze.

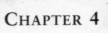

CHAPTER 4

Mrs Hudson

However hard Barry kicked and struggled, the ivy did not let him go. Eventually, he lay still on the floor, covered in dust, wondering if he could take the ivy by surprise.

After a few seconds, he gave a terrific kick and was free. He stood up panting, looking down at the dull green leaves. He had won.

Barry's victory was short-lived. Suddenly he realized that Spot wasn't barking any longer. What could have happened? Was he hurt? Had the ivy hurt him? He had to find Spot fast. Barry was

not only amazed at what had happened
but he was terrified too. Barry was just
about to search the rest of the cottage
when he saw something under the kitchen
table. An ivy-wrapped bundle with a foot
sticking out!

Barry whimpered with fear. He looked
again at the bundle and he screamed and
screamed again!

He saw a shrunken white face and the long grey hair of an old woman. The rest of her was wrapped in deadly tight strands of ivy.

Mrs Hudson never went to Canada. The ivy got her – just as it was going to get him.

Barry didn't notice the long arm of ivy that stretched down from the ceiling until it was too late. It wrapped itself round his throat. At the same time Spot began to howl.

Once again, Barry struggled, grabbing the strands and trying to pull them away. But they only tightened their grip. Using all his strength he snapped each single strand.

Then he was free. But Spot's howl was getting louder and louder. He sounded as if he had never been so terrified in his life.

Pushing his way out into the hall Barry
looked up the stairs. That's where Spot
was – he had to rescue him. He began to
edge his way slowly up, but the ivy was all
over the bannisters. There was a kind of

tunnel, however, and ducking low he was just able to crawl through. His head brushed against the stuff and the rustling sound it made seemed almost like breathing – as if the ivy was alive!

CHAPTER 5

Barry Finds Spot

As he got to the first floor the ivy tunnel became so narrow that he had to push hard against it. What would happen now?

Surely the ivy would strangle him to death.
But Barry had no choice. He had to go on
for Spot's sake. He thought of Mrs
Hudson, lying downstairs, wrapped up
like a bundle, and he gave a little cry of
fear.

But still he pushed on, the ivy catching
and clinging, pulling and tugging at him.

He fought his way along the landing.

"Spot!"

The little dog was whimpering now.

"Spot!"

Then Barry saw him crouching before a half-open door. There was something in there that was making poor Spot terrified. What could it be? Another corpse?

He didn't dare go in. But why should he? All Barry had to do was to grab Spot and somehow struggle back down the staircase. Or maybe a window would be easier, despite the ivy.

"Spot!"

The dog didn't move. Didn't even look round.

"Spot!"

But Spot was still staring into the room through the half-open door, his body shivering, the fur on his neck stiff and spiky.

"Spot!"

It was no good. He would have to go and get him. As he moved forward the ivy rustled louder.

CHAPTER 6

Monster Ivy

Barry charged forward and caught Spot, but the dog jumped out of his arms and ran squealing through the door.

His howling grew louder and the ivy that
was coming through the shattered glass of
the window grabbed Barry round the
waist.

It seemed to push him forward – right
up to the door of the room. And then with
a last shove it sent him inside.

Spot was no longer howling. He was crouched, staring ahead, his eyes fixed on something that Barry could not immediately make out. But the rustling of the ivy grew louder and louder until he could hear the whispered words: "My home now. My home now."

As his eyes finally became used to the dim light, Barry uttered a shrill cry of terror.

The ivy had tumbled through the roof tiles as well as the windows and had formed itself into a figure. Yes, it was a figure all right. And it was alive.

The thing – the ivy thing – had a rustling, quivering, bush-like face with knotty bits for eyes and nose and a dark space for a mouth.

Its gaze was fixed on him, and the mouth was opening and shutting. "My home now. My home now," it whispered.

Barry gazed at the ivy monster in growing horror. But then he thought of poor Mrs Hudson downstairs, bundled into that terrible parcel under the kitchen table.

"Why did you kill her?" he yelled. "She didn't do anything to you."

"I needed to come in."

"You're meant to be outside."

The ivy monster shook its head angrily. "She tried to cut me down. Burn me."

"So she should! You're growing too fast!"

The thing shot out a coil towards him. With panic-stricken energy, Barry grabbed Spot and ran out of that terrible room, burrowing his way down the ivy tunnel, pushing Spot before him.

But with a yelp and a howl, the little dog took off on his own again.

Then Barry felt something catch his foot. He kicked out and was released. But then, as he looked back in terror, he saw the coil of ivy shooting out after him. It was big and strong and woody.

From above he heard a dusty, rustling moan: "It's my home now."

Barry knew that unless he could move faster, the coil would get him. And that would be that.

CHAPTER 7

Caught in the Coils

Twisting and turning, shoving and pushing, kicking and pulling, Barry got through the tunnel. He made it to the kitchen but then the coil caught up with him, twining itself around his neck. It

began to squeeze tighter, and within seconds Barry was finding it difficult to breathe.

He was being strangled.

He went down on his knees, trying to slacken the grip, but it was no good.

More of the coil came down the stairs and he heard rustling laughter from the room above. He could hardly see now.

Everything in the kitchen was a blur and the pain in his head was awful. Then Barry focused on something under the table. The coils of ivy around the body had loosened slightly. In Mrs Hudson's dead hand was a gleaming pair of scissors which he hadn't noticed before.

Barry desperately wondered if he could reach them. Clearly Mrs Hudson had been using a weapon against the ivy too. Now it was his turn. If he could just reach them. But lights were dancing in front of his eyes, his tongue was lolling forward.

The ivy was tightening, tightening all the time. Stretching out his hand as far as he could, Barry just managed to grab the scissors.

With Spot barking in the background, he slashed out at the greedy stems, but with little success. His strength was running out fast. He didn't stand a chance.

Barry dropped the scissors and Spot came up and licked his wrist. The ivy didn't try to harm the dog at all. Slowly a red haze was forming in front of Barry's eyes.

"Spot," he gasped. But how could a dog help him? There came a growling sound and suddenly Spot was tearing at the strands and coils. He was much better than the scissors. Was that a cry of pain Barry heard from upstairs?

Spot's teeth made short work of the ivy and suddenly Barry was free.

Scooping the brave little dog into his arms, Barry ran down the cellar steps and then up and out of the trapdoor.

Panting and gasping, he stood safely in the lane. With Spot clutched tightly in his arms, he watched in horror as the ivy covered the trapdoor. It had finally taken over Mrs Hudson's cottage.